THE TSAR'S RIDDLES

or *The Wise Little Girl*

The TSAR'S

RIDDLES

or *The Wise Little Girl*

Retold from the Russian
by GUY DANIELS

PAUL GALDONE *drew the pictures*

McGRAW-HILL BOOK COMPANY
New York · Toronto · London · Sydney

To Katie,
a very wise very little girl

1435759

TWO brothers were making a trip on horse-back. One was rich, and a bachelor. The other was a poor widower with a little daughter seven years old.

The rich brother's horse, a gelding, was pulling a cart. The poor brother didn't even have a cart —only his horse, which was a mare.

They stopped for the night at a place along the way. While they were asleep, the mare had a colt. As soon as he could get up on his wobbly legs, the little colt tottered over and stood under the cart.

In the morning, the rich man awakened his brother with a shout. "Get up quickly," he exclaimed, "and see what's happened! During the night my cart had a colt!"

His brother got up, saying, "How could it be that your cart had a colt? It was my mare that had the colt."

"You're wrong," the other replied. "If your mare had been the colt's mother, he would have stood under her instead of under the cart."

They took their quarrel to court. The poor brother's arguments were convincing to the judge. But the money the rich brother gave the judge was convincing, too. So the case went from one court to another until it got to the Tsar.

The Tsar had his own way of doing things. When he called the two brothers before him, he said, "Here are four riddles for you. Of all things in the world, what is the strongest and fastest, what is the fattest, what is the softest, and what is the sweetest? Come back in three days and give me your answers."

The rich brother began to think very hard. He didn't think of any answers, but he thought of a friend who might help him.

His friend was an old lady. He went to her house and told her he needed help. She sat him down at a table with good things to eat; and

when he had eaten, she asked him what the
trouble was.

"In three days," he said, "I have to answer four
riddles for the Tsar. First, what is the strongest
and fastest thing in the world?"

"Why, that's easy!" the old lady said. "There's nothing in the world faster than my husband's bay mare. If you just whip her good and hard, she runs as fast as a hare."

"The second question is: What's the fattest thing in the world?"

"I'll tell you—that black-and-white hog we were fattening up last year. He got so fat he couldn't stand on his own four feet."

"The third question goes: Of all things in the world, what is the softest?"

"Why, a featherbed, of course! Anybody knows that!"

"Now this is the last question: What is the sweetest thing anywhere in the world?"

"The sweetest thing anywhere in the world is my little baby grandson, Kolya."

"Thank you, my friend," said the rich brother. "You have been very helpful, and I will never forget it."

When the poor brother got home from the Tsar's palace, his little daughter saw that he was very sad. "What's the matter, Papa?" she asked. "What makes you sigh and cry like that?"

"How can I help sighing and crying? The Tsar has ordered me to answer four riddles that I won't ever be able to figure out."

"What are the riddles?" asked the little girl.

When her father told her, the little girl said, "Papa, you must go back to the Tsar now, and here is what you must tell him.

The strongest and fastest thing in the world is
the wind. The fattest thing is the land, because
it feeds everything that grows and lives on it.

The softest thing is a person's hand, because wherever he lies down he can fold his hands under his head for a pillow. And the sweetest thing in the whole world is sleep."

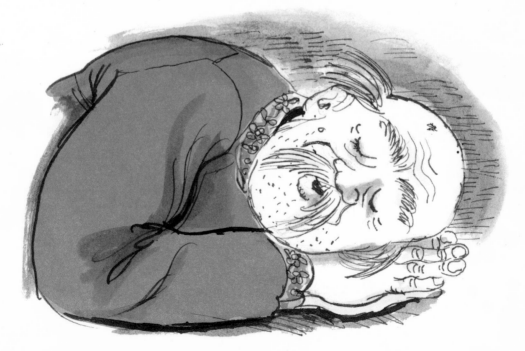

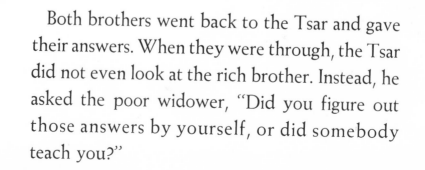

Both brothers went back to the Tsar and gave their answers. When they were through, the Tsar did not even look at the rich brother. Instead, he asked the poor widower, "Did you figure out those answers by yourself, or did somebody teach you?"

"Your Majesty," said the poor brother, "I have
a little daughter seven years old. She taught me."

"I see," said the Tsar. "Well, if your little girl
is so clever, here's something for her to do. Give
her this piece of silk thread and tell her to weave
a fine embroidered cloth for me by morning."

The widower took the little piece of silk thread and went home with it, feeling sorrowful and forlorn. "All is lost," he told his daughter. "The Tsar has ordered you to make an embroidered cloth out of this little piece of silk thread."

"Don't be sad, Papa," the little girl said. She broke off a twig from a branch and gave it to her father. "Take this to the Tsar and tell him to find a workman who can make a loom out of this twig. If he can do that, I'll have something on which to weave the cloth."

Her father told the Tsar. The Tsar listened, and gave him 150 eggs. "Give these to your daughter," he said, "and tell her I command her to hatch 150 baby chicks for me by tomorrow morning."

The widower went home even sadder and more forlorn than ever. "Woe is me!" he cried when he got there. "Now we have gone from the frying pan into the fire!"

1435759

But the little girl just said, "You musn't be so
sad, Papa." She took the eggs and boiled all 150
of them. Then she set them aside for dinner and
supper. "Now, Papa," she told her father, "go
back to the Tsar and tell him the baby chicks
will need a special kind of feed called 'one-day
wheat.' That means the field has to be plowed,
and the wheat planted, harvested, and threshed
all in one day. Tell him that one-day wheat is
the only kind these baby chicks will eat."

When the Tsar heard this, he said, "If your daughter is so clever, let her appear before me tomorrow morning—not on foot and not on horseback, not dressed and not undressed, not with a gift for me and not empty-handed."

"Well," thought the poor widower, "not even my daughter can solve a riddle like that! Now we are indeed lost!"

But when he told her, the little girl said, "Don't be sad, Papa. Run along to the hunter's house and buy me a live hare and a live quail."

The next morning the little girl took off all her clothes and put on a fish net. Then, taking the quail in her arms, she got up on the hare and rode to the Tsar's palace.

The Tsar met her at the palace gate. She got off the hare, and curtsied to the Tsar. "Your Majesty," she said, "here is a gift for you." The Tsar reached out his hands, but the quail flapped its wings and flew away.

"Very good," said the Tsar. "You did everything I commanded you to do. Now tell me: If your father is so poor, how do you manage to eat?"

"My father catches fish on dry land, and I carry them home in my apron and make fish soup."

"What are you trying to tell me, stupid girl! When did a fish ever live on dry land?"

"You're not so smart, either. When did a cart ever have a colt? Colts come from mares, not carts!"

The Tsar ordered his men to give the colt to the poor widower, and he took the little girl to live in the palace. When she grew up, he married her and she became the Tsarina.